Coward-Cowardy Cutlass

First published by A & C Black (Publishers) Limited
Published in Young Lions 1989
9 8

Young Lions is an imprint of
the Children's Division, part of
HarperCollins Publishers Ltd,
77–85 Fulham Palace Road, London W6 8JB

Printed and bound in Great Britain by
HarperCollins Manufacturing, Glasgow

Chapter One

If it had not been for the map,
none of this would have happened . . .

It was long ago and there was
a storm brewing.

The wind was moaning over the cliffs,

the ships were groaning
and creaking
in the tiny
harbour,

and Peter's dad
was moaning
at Peter.

Moan,
moan,
moan.

'Look at the state of this room,' he said. Peter looked at it. It looked all right to him.

Dad was always going on about how wonderful Peter's brother was.

Of course it was all true. Arthur was a right goody-goody.

Arthur ran errands.
Arthur did the washing up
without being asked.
Arthur always wrote
home when he was at sea.

And now Arthur was right-hand man
to Sir Walter Raleigh himself.

Why, even now Arthur is
copying a map for Sir Walter.
But what do you care? You'll never
be anybody's right hand man!

After his dad
had gone,
Peter sulked.

I'll show him. One day
I'll be somebody's
left hand man!

Chapter Two

By the time Peter got up next
morning, Arthur had gone.
Peter was sent up to empty
Arthur's waste-paper bin.
As he picked it up
he noticed something.
Every
scrap of
waste-paper
had the same picture
of the same island,
with the same red cross
on the same spot.

It's a treasure map!

Arthur had taken the best copy for
Sir Walter, but there was nothing
much wrong with these – only the
odd ink blot. This is it, thought
Peter, this is how I'll prove what I
can really do.

Chapter Three

The CRUSTY CROWSNEST tavern
was not a pretty
sight, but it was
the best place to
find a crew, because
only sailors
went there.

Peter marched up to one table after
another, but the reaction was always
the same:

He had almost given up when a big
ugly sailor with a wooden leg and
TERRIBLE breath said to Peter.

If you're lookin' for a
crew, try in that corner—
you're just the sort of
captain they need.
Hur! Hur! Hur!

In the corner was a table, and
sitting around it were some sailors
drinking orange squash.
Peter went across.
'Excuse me,' he said.

Don't creep up on people like that! You gave us the colly-wobbles.

I'm sorry, but someone said that you would let me be captain of your crew

'Oh, did they?' said the sailor, looking sharply across the room.

10

It so happens that <u>I</u> am the Captain of this crew, but I do need a cabin-boy. Do you want the job?

Peter thought.

'All right,' he said.

'Good,' said the captain. 'We sail tomorrow. Bring some biscuits and warm clothes. Goodnight, er . . .'

'Peter,' said Peter the cabin boy.

Chapter Four

Peter stood at the rail of the MERRY WIDOW and looked out across the sea.

So far he was enjoying being a cabin boy. The only problem was that he didn't know where the ship was sailing, or why. If he asked any of the crew they just said:

We don't talk about it.

or

Not now.

or

I'm busy.

In fact it was just like being at home!

Finally, over tea one day, Peter
asked the captain where they were
sailing.

'Ah,' said the captain.
'Ah,' said the captain's parrot.

The captain put a sheet
over the parrot.

ARK!
it's gone
DARK!

Then he spoke
in a low voice.

Actually, we're not sure <u>where</u>
we are going. In this line of work
you have to... well..wait and see.

What line
of work
is
that?

Everybody looked at the captain.

'You'll have to
tell him, Cap'n,'
said Ahab
the bosun.

'Yes, you'll have to,'
said Marco
the cook.

'Tell me what?' said Peter.

The captain squirmed. 'We . . . er
. . . that is . . . um . . . well . . .'

'PIRATES?' Peter hooted with
laughter, 'You lot? *Pirates*?'
The captain looked annoyed.
'What's so funny about that?'
he demanded.

'We've been at sea for only five days.'
said Peter.

"Ahab gets seasick and sleeps with a teddy..."

Marco can't cook because he faints at the sight of blood...

oh dear!

and you're
about as
frightening as an
easter bunny. I'm sorry,
but you're pretty pathetic pirates.'

Funny things began to happen to the captain's face.

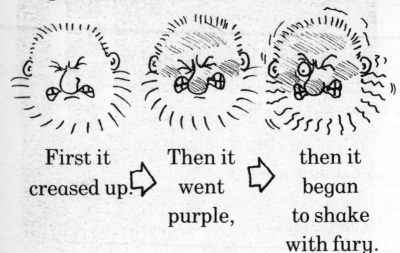

First it creased up. ⇨ Then it went purple, ⇨ then it began to shake with fury.

'Clap him in irons!' he shrieked, 'and throw him into the hold.'

Then maybe he'll learn some manners.

So Peter was bundled into the hold
to wait . . .

in the dark . . .

and the damp . .

for the Pirate Captain.

Chapter Six

Peter did not know how long he had
been in the hold, but even the rats
had gone to sleep.

*I wish I'd never
got onto this stupid ship,
I wish I'd stayed at home,
and most of all I wish...*

We will never know what
Peter wished most of all,
because at that moment
he heard footsteps
clumping down
the ladder.

It was the captain.

'What are you going to do with me?' screeched Peter.

'Please don't yell,' said the captain. 'I'm sorry I had to shout at you. The crew expects it. The fact is,' he went on, 'you were right. We aren't very good pirates.'

I was wondering if you could show us where we're going wrong? It would mean promotion of course. You'd be.. let's see.. First mate!

Keep the noise down!

Gosh.

And that was how First Mate Peter came to be running pirate lessons aboard the *Merry Widow*.

Chapter Seven

'Come on Marco,' said Peter, 'put more snarl into it.'

I've got a sore throat.

'All right,' said Peter, 'that's enough snarling for today. We'll do pirate names instead. Captain, what's your name?'

'Maurice Cuttlethwaite,' said the captain.

Not your **real** name. The name you use when you're pirating.

It's always been Maurice Cuttlethwaite.

'No wonder you don't scare anybody!' said Peter. 'Everybody try to think of a fearsome name for the captain.'

'What's a cutlass?' asked the captain.

'It's a pirate sword,' said Peter.

'You threaten to slit people's gizzards
with it.'

I feel sick!

'I had a cutlass once,' said Ahab. 'I
cut the top off my finger with it.'

Look!

'We must all get cutlasses,' said
Peter, 'but we'll have wooden ones.
That way nobody will get hurt.'

Chapter Eight

A week later, everybody had new names . . .

even the ship.

Captain Cutlass Cuttlethwaite did an hour's shouting practice every morning . . .

He had made a wooden leg too,

and a hook to go over his hand.

It was time to show the captain
the map.

'And if my sums are right,' said Peter, 'the island should be about three days due east.'

'Three days?' said Cutlass Cuttlethwaite, 'then slit my gizzard if we don't go after it, eh mate?'

So the Black Widow set course for the island.

Chapter Nine

Everybody was excited, about the treasure hunt, but they were pirates so they had to pretend to be grumpy.

Then, one sunny morning, Ahab cried from the crow's nest:

Land ahoy!

There was a flurry of activity as a boat was put over the side. The captain, looking his piratical best, stood at the front. Peter sat in the back, grinning as they got nearer . . .

Parrot Pose

Pirate Pose

Pirate Paddle

And nearer . . .

Peter took out the map.

We're looking for 'Dead Man's Hand.'

Let me up! I'm going to be sick!

'It's not a *real* Dead Man's Hand,'
said Peter.
'It's a tree!'

Look!

They ran up the beach,
and began hacking
through the bushes.

I hope this is nobody's garden.

OW! I've got a splinter off my cutlass.

The party reached 'Dead Man's Hand'.
Then as Peter read out directions
from the map, they began to trudge
round the island.

'Are we lost?' asked Marco.

'No,' said Peter, 'this is the spot.
Now, who's got the spade?'

'How can we dig for treasure with
no spade?' shouted Peter.

'I've got a spoon,'
said Marco.
'Will that do?'

They took it in turns to dig with
Marco's spoon. It was hard work,
but the thought of treasure kept
them going.

Then, late on the second day of
digging . . .

They huffed and hauled,

and puffed and pulled,

and at last, with a clunk, they got
the chest to the top of the hole.
Then they opened it.

There was the treasure.

Jewels, brooches, key rings.

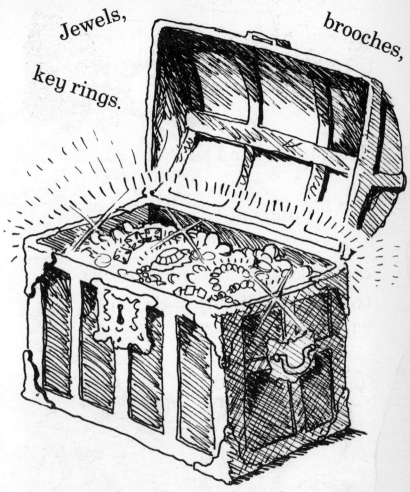

More goodies than they had ever seen.

And it was all theirs.

Chapter Ten

That night on the *Black Widow* they celebrated until way past cocoa time.

Marco danced, Ahab sang, the captain recited poetry,

When morning came, the bleary-eyed crew turned the ship for home. 'Well done Peter,' said Cutlass Cuttlethwaite. 'Thanks to you, we . . .'

He stopped.

His face went white. He began to squeak orders in a high unpiratical voice.

Splice the bilges...er... furl the anchor!

What's wrong?

The captain pointed a shaking hook.
On the horizon was a ship,
and fluttering
from its mast
was the skull
and crossbones.

'Hide me,' pleaded Cutlass
Cuttlethwaite.

'But you're Cutlass Cuttlethwaite
the Fearsome Pirate,' said Peter.
'You aren't afraid of anybody.'

Chapter Eleven

Bloodthirsty Beryl had always had plans for her son Maurice.

Plundering and robbing to pay for his posh schooling, she dreamed of him becoming a lawyer,

or a teacher.

When gossip first reached her of Maurice's embarrassing pirate career, Beryl laughed it off.

But now he was

Cutlass Cuttlethwaite

and he had found treasure. Beryl was

Furious!

'He'll never get into law school now,' she said, turning to her first mate, Hatchet Annie.

'Still,' said Annie, with a wicked grin, 'he has found us some treasure, Beryl.'

Us?

Are you suggesting that we rob my own son?

Yes.

What a brilliant idea!

Bloodthirsty Beryl's ship
raced towards the
Black Widow,
sails billowing.

Arm
yourselves!
We're under
attack!

The crew grabbed weapons and
raced to the side.

'Who are we fighting?' they cried.
'Spaniards? Customs men?
Football hooligans?'

'Bloodthirsty Beryl!' said Peter.

There was a clatter as cutlasses,
sticks and knives hit the deck.

'She's after our treasure,' cried
Peter. 'We can't just let her take it!'

'There must be <u>something</u> we can do!' said Peter.

Chapter Twelve

When Beryl's ship came along side, the *Black Widow* seemed to be deserted.

They've run away.

I'm not so sure — look.

This is what they saw... Isn't it a give-away?

'Maurice,' shouted Beryl, 'come out this minute. Mummy wants to talk to you.'

Shaking, Cutlass Cuttlethwaite
stood up.

Maurice, give mummy the treasure like a good boy.

Speak up Maurice, Mummy can't hear you.

mumble.....

I said 'No', Mum.

She looks frightening

'I'll pretend I didn't hear that,'
Maurice,' said Beryl. 'Now give
Mummy the treasure, or Mummy
will be cross.'

It's our treasure — you can't have it!

There was a
terrible, *terrible* silence.
Then Beryl said, 'Well I shall just
have to come over and take it.'
She was
about
to do
just
that,
when . . .

SPLAT!

a fish landed
right in her hands.

Beryl **hated** fish. Ever since she had been marooned on an island for months with nothing else to eat, the taste, the smell, the SIGHT of fish made her feel . . .

Bleeargh!

Splut

Another fish landed,

Splot

and

another,

A Flying Fish →

Splet!

and another.

Beryl began to turn green.
'Now will you go away, Mother?'
shouted Cutlass Cuttlethwaite.

The pirates of the *Black Widow* rose
from their hiding places, and began
flinging fish with a deadly, pongy,
accuracy. As fast as they threw
them, Marco would supply more
from the galley.

Beryl's pirates tried to dodge the flying fillets but it was no good – they simply slithered and slipped, and got tangled in the rigging

Beryl's ship pulled away and sped towards the horizon, shedding fish.

Just you wait, Maurice... Mummy won't forget this.

The ship became a dot,	then a speck,	and then vanished.

 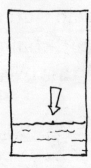 

'Just in time, too,' said Peter. 'We were running out of fish!'

Chapter Thirteen

'Marco's cooking came in useful for a change,' sniggered Ahab.

And I didn't feel sick even once.

'Now then,' said Cutlass Cuttlethwaite, 'what are we going to do with all this treasure?'

'I'm going to retire,' said Ahab, 'and run boat trips round some tropical island.'

'And I'm going to start a cafe,' said Marco. 'I've had enough of piracy.'

'Me too,' agreed the captain. 'It's too much like hard work! I'll just open a little shop. I'll sell fisherman's sweaters.'

Why don't we do it together?

So they did. They found an island,
with a beautiful bay, and they
named it after the captain.

Ahab built a boat,
Marco fed the visitors,
the Captain sold them pirate clothes,
and Peter made maps for people to
hang on their walls.

And that might have been the end
of the story . . .

but it wasn't.

The Last Bit

One day, Sir Walter Raleigh's ship
arrived at Cuttlethwaite's Cove,
And guess who
came ashore?
Peter's brother,
Arthur.

Sir Walter
had just
sailed
a long way
only to find
a treasure island
without a bean
of treasure on it. He was *furious*.

Arthur had been sent ashore to buy
food for the journey home.

Peter took Arthur to
Marco's kitchen,
and gave him a bag of strange,
lumpy vegetables.

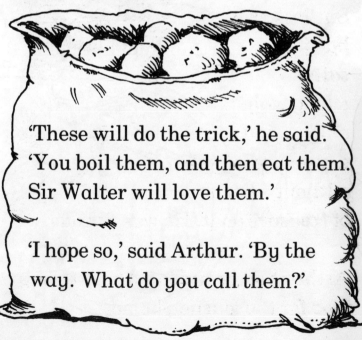

'These will do the trick,' he said.
'You boil them, and then eat them.
Sir Walter will love them.'

'I hope so,' said Arthur. 'By the
way. What do you call them?'

And that is how Sir Walter Raleigh discovered the potato . . .

. . . and how Arthur kept his job!